LEGENDS FROM THE UK

EDITED BY DEBBIE KILLINGWORTH

First published in Great Britain in 2024 by:

Young Writers
Remus House
Coltsfoot Drive
Peterborough
PE2 9BF
Telephone: 01733 890066
Website: www.youngwriters.co.uk

Book Design by Ashley Janson

Softback ISBN 978-1-83565-368-5

Printed and bound in the UK by BookPrintingUK
Website: www.bookprintinguk.com
YB0587DZ

FOREWORD

For our latest competition, The Glitch, we asked secondary school students to turn the ordinary into the extraordinary by imagining an anomaly, something suddenly changing in the world, and writing a story about the consequences. Whether it's a cataclysmic twist of fate that affects the whole of humanity, or a personal change that affects just one life, the authors in this anthology have taken this idea and run with it, writing stories to entertain and inspire. We gave them an added challenge of writing it as a mini saga which forces them to really consider word choice and plot. We find constrained writing to be a fantastic tool for getting straight to the heart of a story.

The result is a thrilling and absorbing collection of tales written in a variety of styles, and it's a testament to the creativity of these young authors, and shows us just a fraction of what they are capable of.

Here at Young Writers it's our aim to inspire the next generation and instil in them a love of creative writing, and what better way than to see their work in print? The imagination and skill within these pages show that we might just be achieving that aim! Congratulations to each of these fantastic authors, they should be very proud of themselves.

CONTENTS

THE STORIES

THE GLITCH

"Imagine the world without the Glitch..."
"Just watch old movies."
"Can't trust them; every record's been tampered with. Speaking of records, have you banked yet?"
"There is still time..."
"Money's tight, I can have only five records banked. How do you even choose five memories to keep from a year's worth before it's all wiped clean?"
"Write down everything you want, it's free."
"A diary? I won't remember about it."
"I'll keep it safe."
"Bank that promise!"
An easy promise to keep. The Glitch didn't bother him; he remembered both great and terrible things that had been long forgotten about.

Zayd Khan (13)

TWO AGAINST THE WORLD

We'd successfully unravelled the puzzle, poised to destabilise the government until James and I awoke engulfed in an eerie black shadow. "What happened?" I exclaimed.

"Uncertain," replied James. It became evident; this was a deliberate move to silence us.

"We've been set up!" we both declared.

James noted, "This was orchestrated to thwart our exposure of the corrupt government."

Trapped, I asserted, "We must leave immediately."

James questioned, "But how?"

After contemplation, we identified our escape route, determined to expose the truth despite being ensnared, ready to defy those attempting to suppress our revelations about the nefarious government.

Bharah Gopal (13)

THE POINT OF MORTALITY

Death knocked on my door one day and asked that I refrain from doing his job for him.
"It is not your time," he said.
I am not sure what I had expected his voice to sound like, but it hadn't been a West Country drawl.
"That's my choice."
"Nothing is your choice," said Death. "Nor is it mine."
"Well," I said, "then what's the point?"
"Of what?"
"Everything," I said. "If I do not dictate the terms of my own mortality then what is the point?"
"The point," said Death, "is to live."
"That's silly."
Death shrugged. "Not my choice."

Felix Shinn (17)

THE HOST

March 2039, and election fever was gripping the citizens of Robovana. Lando Davidson, Peace Party leader, announced his plan publicly.
"I will pledge to win the full support of young people through youth-oriented campaigns," he stated in a televised address.
Ellie, a devoted Catholic, awoke one morning to find what she thought was a bedbug. "Bedbugs aren't metallic..." she pondered.
Upon closer inspection, Ellie found the Peace Party logo on the underside of the supposed 'bedbug'. She called the police.
"Ellie Simonson, this is highly classified information. Your number has been recorded; your words are ours," the pre-taped voice spoke.

Lewis Spackman (17)

GHOST IN THE WATER

"Hold your formation men, they don't see us yet," observed the attentive Admiral Walton, who was leading a small strike force consisting of five of the most advanced stealth submarines the dwindling allied powers had to offer. "We are closing position to the rear of the Soviet's capital sub," continued the Admiral.
Their force was closing in on the Soviet resurgence's most important, and powerful, ship. "Ready!" snarled the stringent Admiral, coming close to a growl... "Aim!" Gone. The Soviet flagship vanished completely from the radar. "Evasive manoeuvres!" yelled the Admiral in a frantic panic. "They have the AI!"

Bobby-James Davis (15)

NEW WORLD

In a tranquil dawn, a glitch froze time. Reality twisted: gravity faltered, buildings contorted. Amid the chaos, innovation bloomed. The world adapted, embracing uncertainty. Fear lingered, but so did wonder. A mishap birthed an extraordinary saga within a hundred breaths - a world reshaped by the glitch's caprice, teetering on possibility's edge. Thrill mingled with terror as society evolved amidst unpredictability. The glitch, a catalyst for change, birthed a new era where ordinary days held extraordinary potential. Each moment, a reminder of the glitch's impact on a world forever altered, trapped between awe and apprehension, reshaping fate in a hundred fleeting heartbeats.

Jessica Rafferty (16)

THE ABYSS

Gone. All gone.

Raylee's distraught scream tore through the sepulchral silence as the ground lurched beneath her. The blade clattered to the ground, and she clamped her hand around her forearm, the skin quickly becoming sticky with the tang of blood. She curled up on herself as Shame hunted for her.

"Leave me alone," Raylee begged, choking on her tears. The relentless laughter grew ever louder, smothering her with hate.

"Freak!"

"Loser!"

"You're just a glitch!"

Another scream was ripped from her heart as the Earth tremored once more.

Everything around her disintegrated into the dark oblivion of her mind.

Emily Ward (17)

ANARCHIC CHAOS

Every clock had stopped... Instantaneously, a 5-minute timer appeared everywhere, on every TV screen, every phone screen, every computer screen and even on the advertising billboards. Everyone's looking around at each other as if to say, "Are you seeing that too?"
Then came, "Simulation ending in 5 minutes," in this android-sounding voice from everyone's phones. Out of nowhere, absolute anarchy ensues. People are fighting, cars are being torched, shops are being raided. Bullets and makeshift Molotov cocktails are flying around like paper aeroplanes. Suddenly, every timer reached 0... Everything is frozen in time, but not the people? And then... darkness.

Matthew Wilkes (18)

LEADING A DOUBLE LIFE

"Night, Winifred!" Mum says softly.
The light switches off and I lie down. Slowly, I drift off with nice thoughts of tomorrow in my head.
"Sandy, wake up!" Raf shouts.
I push him away. It's hard going from Winifred to Sandy.
"I'm telling Mum!"
Hot Australian weather is hard to bear...
"Good on ya!" I shout, rolling my eyes, turn over, pillow over my head and ignore the muffled voices coming through.
Sometimes I wish that I was just Winifred. Wait, I'm falling asleep! Why is Winifred waking up?
"Winifred, darling!" Mum shakes me. "We're going to Australia! Remember?"
Oh no...

Niamh Bacon-Breen (12)

CREATIVE TRANSFORMATION UNLEASHED

On a routine morning, a curious teenager discovered a forgotten journal in the attic. Its pages, inked with forgotten wisdom, revealed a spell to unlock human potential. Sceptical, they muttered the incantation. Suddenly, worldwide, minds ignited with untapped brilliance. Streets buzzed with newfound ideas, and innovation soared. Yet, an unintended consequence emerged - collective consciousness melded, erasing borders and instigating global unity. Governments dissolved, replaced by a harmonious collaboration of minds. The once ordinary world transformed into an extraordinary tapestry of shared dreams, where creativity boundlessly thrived, forever altering the fabric of reality.

Maggie-May Prior (15)

THE DISCOVERY

At the bustling car boot sale, 13-year-old Jake, short and blonde, joined his best friend in exploring. Surprisingly, his friend's mum, an unassuming artist, revealed a unique talent - paintings foretelling the future. Intrigued, Jake discovered destiny's whispers in vibrant strokes. Racing back to school, he persuaded his friend to reconsider the sale. Tension gripped the air as events unfolded precisely as foretold. Grateful, Jake clung to newfound insight. Life's mysteries unfolded daily, guided by artful prophecies. In a world of uncertainty, Jake found solace in a pint-sized mystic and canvases that unveiled the road ahead - his future painted in 100 words.

Ashton Pirie (13)

YOU'RE EARLY...

"You are early," said Death. "What happened, mortal? Your time of death had not reached you yet."
"I came to exchange my soul with my brother's," Ana replied, petrified.
"I beg your pardon?" Death stared at the slim, pale lady, her face shining with determination.
"I will do whatever it takes for Luke," she repeated.
Death hesitated. He summoned a glowing figure with a hand and a river of soul sucked from Ana inhaled with the other. As Luke's form cleared, Ana's soul declined.
"Ana!" Luke cried, staring at the fading image of his beloved sister turning into pure darkness.

Cadence Lee (12)

THE UNKNOWN

They knew it was somewhere here. Near the rotten tree.
Amy stopped suddenly then gasped.
"That's it!" Jeffery exclaimed. They all stopped.
"Are we doing this?" Bob questioned. Without any hesitation, he walked towards the deep crater beyond the rotten tree and peered in. Complete darkness.
Amy held up her hand as if she wanted to stop him but Jeffery calmly took her hand and led her to the edge of the crater, closer to Bob.
"What if..." began Bob.
"We're going in," said Jeffery forcibly.
"It's a portal," Amy said dreamily.
They all nodded and stepped into the unknown.

Daniel Parikos (11)

YOU'RE DEAD? WHAT HAPPENED?

"You're early," Death said confused.
Oliver looked at the man confused as if to ask what he was on about. Eventually, Oliver managed to choke out the words, "W-What?" in a shaky tone.
Death grinned and said, "What do you mean... W-what?" devilishly.
After a few awkward moments, Oliver murmured shakily, "I mean early to what?"
Cheekily Death said, "Hell! You will be given jobs to do during your time here. When you complete them you will be given rewards. If you don't then, well, you'll figure it out.
With that, he clicked his fingers and disappeared. Nothing left. Oliver was left wondering...

Nico Smith (16)

DINNER AND A SHOW

I sat with my dinner in hand, counting down the seconds till the latest episode of my favourite show aired. As the intro played, my heart thumped, dying to see what happened after last week's cliffhanger. As the episode progressed, I noticed the main character behaving... strangely. I ignored it and continued watching.
"Hey. Can you hear me?" a voice called out quietly.
I froze, blood running cold.
Impossible. I live alone. I lifted my eyes towards the screen. The character was staring straight at me.
"What?" I choked out.
With an outstretched hand and desperate eyes, she whispered, "Please... free me."

Kaleece Williams (18)

CHAOS. CONTROL. CONCEIT.

Click. Click.
As the computerised scanner beamed across each student's forehead, the school hall echoed with shrieks of agony. Like dazed soldiers stunned in silence, the students instantaneously marched towards the hall door - they were moths hovering towards the nearest source of light. The students' cold expressions swigged by the click of a button. Wafts of the school's fish and chips mingled through the corridors as the students proceeded to their dormitories - arms by their sides and stone faces. With ease, the group of students were partitioned into social classes.
Who was controlling them? What would happen now...?

Muhammad Rahman (11)

A BEAUTIFUL NIGHT

The moon drowned beneath a hive of obscure mist. Intent emerged dilated, wild pupils. Fingers played an unseen piano; creating unimaginable music. For ears invisible lowered beneath vitreous waves. Claws clawed scrap clothing clinging by the closing channel. Slithering slime settled upon sinking figures. The night was unending, the stretch of waters unbending. Children's cries echoed down - screeching unearthly with paining power.

"Is this what faces humans in the future?"

Jesus closed his fists and the vision was gone.

"It will be a beautiful night when our malevolent God shall be upon them. Why do you look so sad?"

Runyi Liu (16)

THE GLITCH

65 million years ago, the sky was red, dinosaurs were running havoc around the Earth. A meteor was falling out of the sky. Suddenly... the meteor stopped. It started shaking and disappearing. Reappearing and finally disappearing. The dinosaurs confused carried on life normally, till the present day.
Present day... "Run T-rexes are coming," yelled a woman.
"What happened back then? Why are the dinosaurs still here? What happened to the meteor?" Joe said.
"No one knows, apparently it glitched out of existence and they didn't die but we still evolved," I said. "But we are here and we must survive."

Jacob Penfold (12)

TWO UNIVERSES, ONE BOY

Phillip rushed through the streets, panting heavily. His mum would kill him if he was late for family games night. Dashing through a dark alley, Phillip noticed something strange. That brick in the wall cast no shadows! Slowly, Phillip reached forward and touched it.
Bang! Phillip lay, resting on the grass. He was confused. Grass does not usually grow in alleyways. Sitting up, Phillip looked around. He was in a completely different area.
"What happened?" said Phillip, confused.
"You glitched between universes," said a voice behind him. "And unless you fix it, you'll be ripped apart by reality."

Henry Giles (11)

SUMMER'S REGRET

The cold wind blew into Summer's face, tears rolled down her cheeks, falling into the long grass. The moon glimmered as Summer asked, "You mean, she's gone?"
"I'm so sorry, baby, the doctors can't do anything."
"Mum, is this a joke? Car crash, really? My six-year-old sister, this is a joke, right?"
Summer felt like a dagger had just sliced through her heart, but there was nothing she could do about it.
"This isn't a joke, baby, she knows we love her, so much."
"Mum, I told her she was the worst." She looked up into the starry sky. "I'm sorry."

Millie Gidney (11)

THE START OF SCARLET'S STORY

It's five years since the planet exploded. Today we can step out to see what's left.
"I want to go out," Lily said.
"You must stay by my side," Scarlet said.
Nature was covered in a glowing essence. That's when Lily picked up this glowing rock.
"Don't touch!" Scarlet said, mesmerised by its beauty. She picked it up, cracked it open accidentally, in it was a small crystal. That's when they heard 'it'.
The screeching sound of creatures. Scarlet's arms started to glow a dark blue colour, absorbing the crystal's magic. She realised nothing would be the same again.

Soffia Lloyd Jones (14)

THE SWAP

I didn't move, but my reflection did. I tried masking my shock by feigning amusement.
"Who are you and what are you doing in my room?" I queried.
"I'm *you*, can't you see?" my reflection shook with laughter. It even had my voice!
"Come a little bit closer!"

I did as I was told. Now I was just an arm's length away from the mirror. My reflection seemed astounded by my sudden obedience.
The following happened so swiftly, I couldn't prevent it. In an instant, we both swapped places. My reflection laughed at my foolishness.
"Now, who is the outsider here?"

Emilia Kaczorek (14)

THE GLITCH

In the middle of the computer world (the matrix), 'The Glitch' appears and confuses everyone. Something strange happens in the digital world, messing up the usual way things work. Imagine pixels acting crazy, like they're in control of something and fighting back.
In this mix-up, a hero appears - a person who writes the instructions for computers. As these instructions get all blurry, the world they're in starts to break apart, showing hidden secrets.
'The Glitch' is like a magic doorway, bringing both danger and opportunity.
It's a journey through a world of computer stuff that challenges what we know.

Ekko Merkuriy Zarayskiy (12)

THE FINAL BOUGH

In the darkest hour of humanity's existence, the trembling hands of Man wielded their axes against Mother Nature herself, mercilessly slashing away her ancient roots. The deafening thud of falling timber reverberated through the desolate landscape, drowning out any remaining semblance of life. With every felled tree, a desperate gasp escaped from our planet's very lungs, pleading for mercy from an apathetic universe...
The final tree was cut down, and with it vanished the last vestiges of precious oxygen. In this cataclysmic moment, mankind sealed its own grim fate, consigning itself to an airless abyss where breath ceased to exist.

Hafsa Muhammad Nusair (12)

DEATH'S GAME

She had no choice; this had to be done. Stepping half-heartedly towards the arena, she peered inside. A dull hall not at all lightened by the figure's lifelessness. Death. She swallowed, attempting to chip at the log in her throat. *Just do it,* her mind screamed. Suddenly, her hand was swinging towards it. It penetrated through the heart. A hologram. A glitch in reality. The thought plunged into her mind, sending ripples of shock through her body. "You should know better than to cheat death," said a voice, "the consequences haunt humanity."
She turned, screamed, but no sound... silenced eternally. Death.

Bramiya Kugathas (12)

DEATH'S MERCY

"You're early," said Death. "What happened?"
"The wrong place, the wrong time, the wrong person." That was all that needed to be said. Death only sighed as he observed the mortal plain below from the spiritual heights of the afterlife, staring judgment down onto the severity of my fate.
"You had more to live for," the spectre said.
I nodded in response. "Take me home," I pleaded.
The spectre obliged solemnly. The dark haze of death surrounded me. I looked upon the spectre one more time, unspoken words lingering between us. I'll be back soon. Death always sets me free.

Grace Evans (17)

LOVED BY DEATH

The angel of death stands before me, an ethereal being, the most captivating ever witnessed, gracing me with its melodic voice.
"This is unusual; I have been dispatched to retrieve you, human, yet I believe it's not your appointed hour," it spoke in an elegant, slow-paced manner. "I shall return to my sender and plead for an extension of your time."
Words elude me as I struggle to fathom its radiance. Its illusory structure, surpassing any man, would have that effect on any being attempting to comprehend the entity.
"You see, human," it continued, "I find myself enamoured with you."

Saja Hussein (14)

HELP! CAN YOU HEAR ME? OH WAIT...

'We were Batch-42. We were the last resort. We were-'
The entry ends. Oh well, everyone knows what happened.
We were oblivious when the first mutations came; we were all unaffected. It was only three hours later when the news articles were written, did we read them? Well, some of us didn't, they couldn't see anymore. Senses were being lost. The grimmest was losing touch, their skin flaking then dropping.
We who were safe from the mutation weren't from society; they hurdled us up as a recruitment effort to find a cure. Too bad they were on the last batch.
"Help! Can you hear me, Oh wait..."

Siya Patel (15)

THE REFLECTIVE REPTILE

I didn't move, but my reflection did.
Its eyes, once mirrors of my own, now gleamed with a malevolent hunger. A sinister grin twisted its features, foretelling the horror. Panic.
It clenched my throat as the reflective surface rippled, releasing a grotesque monster that took shape with predatory intent.
Frozen, I witnessed my doppelgänger's transformation into a nightmarish beast, its claws extending toward me. The room echoed with a menacing growl, and as the monstrous reflection lunged, I grasped the danger concealed in each reflective surface. This secret devoured those who dared to meet their own gaze.

Thomas Lin (11)

THE MALFUNCTION

I'm winning!" said Berry. We were sitting in the living room playing Battle Crusades and everything was going normally until 'it' happened. We were transported through the TV to another world, one of dilemmas.
At first, we were having fun but that quickly changed, this was not reality. "Wow! robots," said Jack.
"Maybe there's aliens too?" said Berry.
Everyone looked at us disapprovingly. A robot and an alien approached us, we were worried. What were they planning to do? They took us to a prison and summoned us to a battle of games. We then got transported back. Was this a game?

Charmya Hardy (12)

UNBOTHERED

I sighed loudly enough to annoy my mother and collapsed into the airbed. It deflated, air hissing from somewhere. I was unbothered.
Then the ground fell in. I felt myself flying, flailing, falling... Which way was up? I didn't know anymore. I eventually slowed, falling dreamily, until I was bobbing in a body of water.
I assumed I was dreaming - then my mother came crashing down, spluttering and thrashing. I looked around calmly as she yelled various profanities. We were in a cave with glittering, purple stalactites and fireflies swimming patterns in the tingling, magical air.
I sighed again, unbothered.

Ruby Tildesley (16)

THE WORLD WENT QUIET

I couldn't hear myself think. The screaming. The crying. The running. My mind was a labyrinth of bewilderment.
The sound of screaming grew even more intense, reaching a deafening crescendo. And suddenly, there was complete silence, as if the world held its breath. Every clock had stopped. Every human had stopped. The screams, the cries, the running. It all went quiet, yet I found myself inexplicably propelled forward, defying the eerie silence that enveloped everything else...
I gasped in pure shock. The screaming. The crying. The running. It all had arrived again. And suddenly the world went quiet. Once again...

Khloe Ndjoli (14)

WHISPERS OF TIME

In the quirky town, an eerie event unfolded - all the clocks stopped. Benny sensed something extraordinary and found himself drawn into the mystery. As the frozen clocks cast a mysterious calm, whispers of hidden surprises grew louder. Benny embarked on a journey to unravel the enigma, each step bringing him closer. Unbeknownst to him, deeper mysteries veiled the answers. The quirky town held its breath as Benny delved into the silent ticking of the frozen timepieces. In the shadows, the mysterious old man Elias watched, his ancient eyes reflecting a silent understanding of the secrets woven into the fabric of the frozen time.

Eden Hinman (14)

STAIRWAY TO HEAVEN

I woke up in a lift.
It didn't seem like an ordinary lift. It was made of glass, which on its own wouldn't have seemed that strange, but the glass allowed me to see that this particular lift was steadily rising through thin air. A man with wings stood in the corner, holding a clipboard. 'Stairway to Heaven' echoed from an invisible speaker.
The man looked up. "You're awake!" he smiled. "Welcome to Heaven, Rose."
"My name's not Rose," I said, frowning.
His smile dropped. "Oh no."
He snapped his fingers. In an instant, I was back in my bed.

Saoirse Williams (15)

WHISPERS IN THE VOID

Surrounded by an oppressive sea of white - walls, sheets and an unsettlingly pristine toilet seat - desperation sets in. A snicker, hoarse and distant, emerges through steel bars that offer a narrow view into an identical cell. "How do I escape?" I demand, my hands clenching the cold steel. His unseen figure responds cryptically, "Escape?" He chuckles, "You're hopeful now, but despair claims everyone. Eventually, you'll be lost in time, like me." He rises into view and horror seizes me at the sight. The urgency to escape intensifies, yet the mystery of our shared situation deepens.

Sama Hussein (16)

THE TALE OF TURRIM MORI

3pm on a Tuesday afternoon on a hot London day. It all started normal enough, a couple of trembles in the water, nothing noticeable. But at around 3.30, waves started appearing out of nowhere. Around 5 minutes later, it appeared. A gargantuan head with 2 horns appeared from the horizon, its size blocking out the sun. The temperature dropping to freezing in seconds. Suddenly, the beast's hand, or what at least substituted as one, rose from the ocean and smashed right into the London Eye, sending it across the city causing mass destruction. God's punishment personified, the divine destroyer of the cosmos, Turrim Mori.

Dylan Elhasham (14)

THE YEAR FUSER

The morning of the 10th of January 2098 had been uneventful. Elijah had got ready for school and headed out. Later that day, it would change.
While finishing his homework after school, a tiny barely noticeable crack shook his apartment floor. A frantic array of colours encased half of his room. The now enclosed half swiftly deteriorated away, revealing the other side of the room. Elijah glared at something strange. A calendar. That said: '10th January... 2023'.
Then, someone entered the room. He sat down and took out his notebook. Elijah's mouth gaped open. The notebook said: 'The Year Fuser'.

Wan Razin Bin Wan Armizi (12)

THE CLICK THAT WIPED OUT A SPACECRAFT

My fingers trembled as I raced them gently over the keys.
The potential benefit of Project Xenia was plentiful but if anything didn't go to plan, all the people boarding the KamWel craft would perish, including me.
I shook at the thought, but it wasn't enough to stop me activating the risky software.
I weighed up the benefits and dangers of carrying on with the project, and I came to the unreliable conclusion that activating MJYG-based software couldn't be disastrous enough to kill.
Without thinking, I clicked the button, and before I knew it, everyone perished, and everything fell apart...

Samiya Aleena (11)

THE TIP OF THE ICEBERG

These drawings predicted the future. Overcome with childish glee, Ed Smith beamed at himself, kitted out in navy blue and white. A captain! So, that's what he was to be! Delighted, he eagerly flicked through illustrations of lavish master cabins and pearl-adorned ladies fawning for a dance. Suddenly his fingers faltered. Gone were the champagne flutes and caviar, replaced by chilling images of frenzied stampedes and men overboard. Trembling, Ed flipped the final page, etched with the date '1912'. Only just discernible: a ship bow falling into the depths. What had happened? Or rather, what was going to happen?

Annabel Sadler (17)

THE GLITCH

I didn't move but my reflection did.
Everything was in black and white including my reflection which was gargantuan but weirdly shaped, that's when I realised I wasn't a normal human being.
Abruptly my reflection changed in size from gigantic to minuscule and so on, all I know is that I wasn't dreaming, everything was real.
The reflection was slowly consuming me, becoming more and more powerful, taking over my body, until my shadow became twice as big as my height.
That's when out of nowhere a weird light came and shone, bringing everything back to normal making everything normal.

Hassam Hussain Ali (18)

THE SECRETS BEHIND HER EYES

Finally, his creation was done. He stood back and gazed at it. My 'AI Ally' he called it. Reaching out, he clicked the iridescent button on her back, and the robot lit up, coming to life. "Hello." Grinning maliciously to himself, he ambled off, glancing at her once more in admiration.
Ding! The bell on the door tinkled, signifying a customer had come in. Jake gasped at the exquisite robot. Examining it a little closer, his eyes widened. The robot's eyes flickered. They were unmistakably human. Tears streamed down her metal face. "Leave. Leave now before it's too late..."

Abiha Fatima Baig (12)

REVENANT

The first few minutes were effortless; a children's prank, a nervous joke and then a piercing panic. This is no peaceful slumber. There has been a failure, a miscarriage in nature.
When will the seventh trumpet sing?
To escape this putrid foaming, I would warmly lay beneath sheet upon sheet of flame, plead pain to lick over these undead bones, assemble horned audiences to taunt!
Unheard screams are those most wretched; I, with liquid cerebrum, ruminate this thought, while some false agony pulsates my rotting cavity. My cold bed shudders once again under soil.
We, alone, feel each neighbour calling...

Anna Lennox (18)

THE GLITCH

Alone in her apartment, Lily's routine shifted upon finding a forgotten watch on her route to work. Clasping it onto her wrist, an inexplicable energy enveloped her. Fatigue set in; during a break, panic struck seeing coworkers frozen in mid-action. Desperation clawed at Lily as she tried removing the watch - it resisted, emitting a sonorous hum.
Suspense lingered as Lily grappled - an unyielding watch, a frozen world, and the promise of a glitched existence. The weight of her decision pressed, and an unsettling mix of fear and curiosity churned, leaving Lily on the precipice of a reality-altering choice.

Chinemerem Gabriella Egbeogu (12)

HOW DEATH DIED

"Why won't you die?" Death accuses her.
When she doesn't answer, he snarls at her, "Earth's living time is up. I'm the living being that will never die."
He raises his sword to strike, but he's choking on the blood-rain that he sent down to Earth to kill everything. But now he's dying and so is everyone else. She should be too, but she stays breathing as blood drips down Death's silver armour and he dies and she's left to watch as everything just disappears.
She watches as Death and everything else dies, and she is just left there, alone. Alive.

Hargun Kaur (14)

REALITY

Sometimes I feel like I exist outside of the realms of reality.
An ineffable longing to feel everything a normal person does, yearning to feel something, anything.
Constantly examining the way someone's face twists in agony, how someone's expression crinkles in pure happiness, or how a person's eyes illuminate with joy, staring endearingly at someone they love.
It's ironic, I know all of these small, unspoken things, whilst I have no ability to display them myself.
Maybe the one thing I do feel is an alien desire to be something I'm not.
A glitch in human normality.

Emily Phinn (13)

PARASITE CITY

Damien, is a 15-year-old boy from Parasite City. His hometown has horrifying backgrounds to uncover. An evil parasite had hit the City in 1996. Destroyed all and had disappeared.
28 years later, the same strange things have been happening again. There was a mine. Damien entered the old coal mine and found a dusty book, no wonder the authorities never let anyone in, there were secrets. He opened the book, it was blank. All of a sudden, it started writing... 'It's the end of the road... Damien'. Damien then got sucked in.
"You're early," said Death. "What happened?"

Winter Harte (11)

THE RAPTURE

Angels. So many angels. Pedestrians walked down the dusty streets, utterly oblivious to the divine beings that shadowed them. Some angels had huge, pure, feathery wings. Others trailed idly behind their humans as if they'd given up hope of trying to change them. She saw one following a baby in a stroller - an unbelievably vast angel, made up of interlocking, ever-rotating golden rings with countless piercing eyes and wings emblazoned on it, white light blaring so brightly, she could scarcely look at it any longer. She gazed skywards, only to see an infinite flock descending the heavens. It was happening.

Aurelia Littlejohn (15)

THE BOY WHO WAS ALIVE

After a long workday, Marcus relaxed with Netflix until 1am, then hit the hay at 1:05am. In a bizarre twist, he encountered a ghostly doppelganger, prompting an unsuccessful call for help from his dad. The next day intrigued and uneasy, Marcus delved into his house's history, discovering haunting tales. Collaborating with paranormal experts, he identified a lost spirit seeking closure. Through a heartfelt connection, Marcus assisted the ghost's transition, transforming his once eerie home into a serene haven. He then sold his house because he didn't want to live in fear for the rest of his life.

Jashwanth Karthikeyan (13)

SIMULATED

It started about a month ago. And I can't take it anymore.

At first, they were small things: the sound of the sea when I looked at a fishbowl; cries of crows from seagulls. Then, the same phrases: "Lovely day out." "How're you?" Same tone, same voice.
The world... what's happening? Another woman goes past, that default expression on her face. Is any of this real?
A voice, choked-up and heavy with desperation, cries down from the sky, "I'm sorry... the day you died... I couldn't just leave you there. Cassie, forgive me - I made this for us."

Inka Stephenson (16)

THE GLITCH

"The drawings predicted the future," I whispered dumbfounded. My older sister, Rebecca, looked at me incredulously, shaking her head profusely. Becca was petrified; she'd seen the drawings and she hated them. But they were true. The virus took over and engulfed everything in its wake. We had to stop it! Gingerly, we crept out of the house and into Becca's car. Becca was a scientist and I wanted fun. Covertly, we crept into the obsolete lab. An earthquake of disgust shook our cores as we uncovered the truth. That virus was no accident; it was maliciously created to eradicate humanity...

Godfrey Oseki (14)

WHAT IF IT GETS ONE DEGREE HOTTER EVERY MINUTE?

I'm at the playground, it suddenly gets exceedingly warm, it's usually 2°c, no more. I went home to put my shorts on. Suddenly it was on the news, "It's 25°c in Iceland."
Now the elderly began dropping dead right in front of my eyes, there were now only 300 individuals alive in Iceland. I was perched in the shower bawling my eyes out, all my family members had passed.
Minutes went by, it was now 43°c, there was nothing we could do about it.
Seven minutes later... I was the only one in Iceland. I was throwing up.
I'm passing away by the second.

Alethea Cliffe (12)

LET'S GO FOR A HIKE!

It was a warm, breezy morning. Mirabelle was chilling in bed until her mum stormed in. "Mirabelle, we're going for a hike."
"Urgh!" she moaned. She got up, got dressed, downed her breakfast and off her family went.
After a long morning, they had only managed to get halfway up the mountain until... *Bang!*
Thunder flashed and banged in front of their eyes. The rain shortly followed, and the blue sky turned black. What would they do? "Gosh!" her dad shouted. They all took shelter until the storm passed. But didn't that mean it was night-time?

Maisey Lee (11)

THE GLITCH

The rich golden Chocolate bar stood out into my pure eyes as my taste buds watered and tingled in need. I unravelled the milky delicious chocolate and snapped a precious piece off. My friends stared at me as I softly shut my eyes and bit down on the chocolate in delight! My taste buds released joy. Ten seconds later something mysterious began to happen. I was oozing out chocolate everywhere! I was becoming a chocolate fountain! My eyes popped
out and my hair was like sopping spaghetti! My friend looked horrified! "What's happening? What's happening? This must be a big glitch!"

Millie Barnaby (13)

SILENCE

On a normal Wednesday, in the city of London, something was wrong. Something was very wrong. There were no lights. No computers, no phones, no people on the street, no internet. No communication at all.
London wasn't alone in experiencing this shock. Similar scenes emerged throughout the world. Russia, Turkey, France and all countries experienced the same shock.
People couldn't talk to each other, verbally or online. The internet was down, and everyone's vocal cords were down as well. No one could talk or communicate. This was very wrong.
Then, everyone's lives changed...

Muhamed Yahye Ali (11)

THE BUTTERFLY EFFECT

I caved. I got the app, just like my mates. Everything is normal, why was I so paranoid? Wait... Is that my father?... He survived? But... okay, whatever. I walked around, like normal. Everything looks normal. I looked up. Where did the sky go? Why is it... glitching?... Black? No. Red? I continued my walk, my pace quickening. My dad is here and now my best friend. I'm so confused. 'We will meet again'. Why is that all I can see? I am really scared... Is this what the butterfly effect feels like?
"You're early," Death said, confused.
"I'm early?"

Alastair Birch (16)

HEY...

As Dave woke up he looked around the white room. He saw this man in all black and he said to Dave, "You're early."
"Who are you?" Dave said shaking.
"I am Death," Death replied with a calm voice.
"Where am I and what happened?"
"You died, no easy way to tell you, you're dead," replied Death in a sympathetic tone.
"Why is it always me, Death? How did I die?" Dave said, crying his eyes out.
"Well, you were leaving your mum's house and a man came up to you and said, "Hey..."."

Tyler Revell (15)

FORTUNE

"I'll grab the paper," Pippa said while Florence got some pens.
Luke folded the paper, scribbled down a few fortunes and handed it to Florence to colour in. "Finished!" they shouted, handing it back to Luke.
Luke grabbed it and Pippa sat next to him. He picked a colour and a number and eventually got his fortune. "You'll get run over by a bus!"
Pippa giggled. They laughed all night until morning when Luke decided to go to the shop. He crossed the road and a horn beeped frantically.
We never saw him again because of that stupid game...

Lottie Cooke (13)

GONE

Things had felt strange for a while now, people going missing, unexplained tragedies and deaths... like... a glitch. Something that was there and then, well, wasn't. I wasn't going to worry about it at first but now I'm not sure. I got up the other day, and that's when... 'it' happened. I looked in the mirror and there was some sort of shadow standing in the back. I turned around, terrified, but it wasn't there, then again two minutes later but when I turned around... I was in the same place except it wasn't. It was burned crisp and... gone. I'm trapped.

Aimeè-Grace Stevens (16)

DOOMED

Suddenly the young girl was forced awake by a chorus of noise. She pulled herself to the window and glanced down at cars blaring, screams of horror and people walking confused upon the streets. One of them was supposedly her dead grandma. *Am I hallucinating?* Other people shrieked as they left their houses and pulled a passerby into their arms, shouting. What was happening? The news suddenly switched on and the man on the screen was sweating profusely as he spoke... "Everyone dead on Earth... is now alive!" was all she heard before she blocked out everything else... What?

Ayesha Siddiqah Ahmed (16)

NOT ENOUGH OXYGEN LEFT

I won't stop, I can't stop. There's not enough left. Legs aching, heart plummeting, not enough left. Gasping for air but there is not enough left. Dizzy and tired, all I know is it is over; there's not enough left. I can feel the air being sucked out of my lungs, my throat coarse. Oxygen rising, flying away, along with my life. Up, up, high - to a place that could never be described. Never. Where the oxygen now lies. Where I will finally rest.
"Nooo!" I shrieked.
One last desperate cry into the void. But it's not enough, there's not enough left.

Isobel Ellson (13)

INVADED

Green, formless limbs, a huge head accompanied with half-friendly, half-creepy bulging eyes that somehow rest perfectly on a disproportionate body - but this is none of that? This being?... Or thing?... Or something like that has no counterparts, no relations, nothing in our reality I or we have ever seen that we could compare it to.
It's clear that the rumours are true - though they're never first-hand accounts. Those who are unfortunate enough to catch the terror-filled gaze of this thing never live to tell the tale. Those rumours are true too.
Earth is no longer ours.

Jayden Kurankye (16)

ARE YOU MISFUNCTIONING?

The sun hadn't risen for five years. However, I was in no hurry for it to. My friend told me to download this app. However, it gave me many warnings but I still downloaded it. In a puff of smoke, I was transported! My brain tingled as I realised what lay before my hazelnut eyes. A city! But with broken lampposts, cracked windows and even smashed houses. Aside all this I kept walking. I finally reached a mysterious shed. It looked grim however I still walked in. "We've been expecting you..." someone said. Suddenly the door slammed behind me and I realised I was trapped...

Aiva Elizabeth Bino (11)

FALLING

Staring out of the cylinder-shaped window, I was confronted by the sun's blinding rays of light which were illuminating the pale sky. Snow-white mountain tops below, trust through the clouds. All of a sudden, there was an ominous light, which banged in the distance, like a firework on Bonfire Night. I looked away, afraid. Once peeking back, there appeared to be a disc-shaped aircraft, hovering in the air. Something like a bullet was shot towards the plane, black swiggles spread around the interior. Red flashes, error signs and beeping noises sprung in every corner. We were... falling.

Sara Chauhan (12)

SOUNDLESS DAYS

In a world governed by a cruel decree, Faye, like all women, could only utter a mere fifty words a day. Her voice, a precious commodity, was held captive by an oppressive male regime, that thought of women as mere accessories. Faye was forced to navigate life in silence, forbidden to express her thoughts. In the quietude, she discovered the power of selective words, weaving intricate tales with brevity. A group of exasperated women planned to rebel. Faye, their muse, dared to dream of a voice unshackled. Through coded gazes and whispers, rebellion brewed. The battle for words had begun...

Kishani Suresh (13)

ONE CLICK

It's just the enter key, just one delicate press of a key; a click away from the current of the Earth's steady stream to shift. One minuscule, insignificant movement - one minuscule, insignificant person - completely altering reality in its entirety. Just. Press. The. Enter. Key. Who knew such a small decision could adjust the fates of the universe so tremendously? Ironic.
Click.
Code Successful, Running Program.
Panic, wailing, screaming, traitors, tears, misfortune, curses, anger, crime. Darkness. Depression. Death... Secrets... Chaos... forever...?

Mandy Dai (13)

SKIMMING STONES

We were in the wrong place at the wrong time. Skimming stones on the wrong lake on the wrong summer evening, the air humid and stifling.
We stood waist-deep in the water for a respite from the oppressive heat. Captivated, I stared down at my distorted reflection, the others following suit, their faces blank. That should've been the first sign something was wrong.
The lake rippled where my fingers met the water. Then suddenly, my reflection moved, lurching forward, as a hand, a solid, fleshy, slimy hand broke the surface of the water, grabbing my wrist and dragging me under.

Amelia McMillan (14)

REVENGE IS A DISH BEST SERVED COLD, OR SHOULD I SAY - WET?

Drip. He pounded resignedly on the coffin door. Mocking laughs muffled from above, hers stood out, different from others. He had not heard her for many years yet the mockery and eeriness of it remained glued to him. Forever embedded in his memory. *Drip. Drip. Drip.* The sound of water grew persistent, his body slowly submerging underneath it. As the coffin filled, he wondered; *how it was, that she was up there and he was five feet under, the roles should - were - reversed.* He'd been sure she was dead, now it seemed he'd be the one to meet death first.

Abigail Ikuesan (14)

EARTH'S FINAL ERA

Time tapped the alarm clock. Strange. It should have gone off by now, like every morning. He crossed the room, listening for the ticking of the grandfather clock. Silence. He peered out the window and was met with thick, unyielding fog. Impenetrable, eternal gloom. The sun would not rise. He had seen this before. Time sighed. How could this era of life on Earth be over?

"It wasn't meant to happen so soon," he lamented.

"Still, I don't believe the humans were meant to last. I can only hope life will find a way." He clicked his fingers. Blackness.

Holly Hutcheon (16)

FLUENT

Getting thrown into Pulse City wasn't easy.
Boots didn't know how to feed herself or navigate the meandering alleyways.
Walking around where she lived would make anyone apprehensive with its dizzying lights and the threat of attack at any point, but for Boots it was normal.
She had a knack for talking, getting her way with words instead of her actions, but just as she was finally settled in this null, she lost it all because of a Silver.
A chip that corrupts your greatest strength: your voice.
Now she was back to square one again... back in danger.

Thomas Stroud (14)

LOST AND FOUND...

In the dimly lit alley, shadows danced ominously against the graffiti-covered walls. The air was thick with anticipation as I hurried my way through the labyrinthine streets. Heart pounding, I turned a corner and collided with a stranger. Our eyes locked for a fleeting moment, and in that instant, I sensed a strong correlation. But before I could utter a word, the stranger vanished into the night, leaving me with a burning curiosity and a trail of unanswered questions. Little did I know, this encounter would unravel a web of secrets that would forever change the course of my life.

Muhammad Yunus (12)

LOST IN THE NIGHT

It was dark and cold. I was walking home from a long shift. I walked for what felt like hours and didn't find myself getting any closer. I checked the time... '10:34pm'. It had only been four minutes since I started walking. I continued walking, I quickly realised I was walking in circles, seeing the same houses. I noticed shadowy figures around corners. I was unsure what was going on, but I'd been walking for what felt like four days, the sun hadn't risen and my clock hadn't changed.
I hadn't seen another soul except for the ones following me...

Maddie Kikkert (16)

ERASED

Mary was on her laptop but suddenly a message popped up. It said: 'Virus detected'. The girl clicked the button that said: 'Remove virus'. Little did she know she was making a huge mistake.
Kim walked into the bedroom. "Have you seen your father anywhere? He said he was going shopping, it's like he just vanished."
Mary's eyes widened. Did she erase her dad from Earth just by clicking one button? Where did he go?
Mary got up and ran downstairs into the living room to the photos above the fire, her dad wasn't in them anymore...

Macy Rasmussen (16)

TOMORROW'S HERE

She was the last one. She had been for days. The moon hung high in the sky, creating menacing shadows from the tall trees above. Birds sang eerily, mocking her fear. Perhaps it was the pounding of her heart or the cold sweat that had broken out against her body but, she knew she wasn't alone.

"Tomorrow," she repeated to herself as she trekked through the forest. The leaves crunched beneath her feet but this time she noticed something. She stopped. Waiting. Listening. The echo wasn't real, there was somebody mimicking her steps. A cold hand gripped her...

Angelrose Ugwu (15)

GLITCH

12am, that's the time. I should be asleep but the sunlight streaming through my open curtains makes it impossible to drift off. I climb out of bed and over to them, pulling them shut against the blinding light. Wait... the light... from the sun... that should have set hours ago!
I quickly turn on the TV, the first words I see are 'Panic' and 'Fear'. Apparently, I wasn't the only one who noticed this... glitch... Pictures flash of car crashes bathed in midsummer light and people rushing home in terror. I know only this: the world we know has ended.

Ellie Bartles-Smith (13)

DRAGONS

The middle of the night, normally quiet, when people sleep, relax. Not tonight because tonight fairytales and real-life join. Reality breaks and imagination takes over.
Hours passed by and people became increasingly bored and cold. Just as they were leaving, a small crackling noise coming from the sky got louder and the dark midnight sky turned orange like the middle of a flame and the cold crisp air turned hot and humid. The sky began to rip in half revealing dragons, dangerous, fire-breathing, people-eating dragons but can we live in peace or is it the start of war?

Amber Musker (13)

THE REALM OF THE GLITCH

It's empty. The world, once bursting with various forms of life, love, and spontaneity, is replaced with a realm of the void. Silence. No bustling of fresh green leaves on the tops of the tallest trees; no calming chirps of birds gliding through the boundless bright blue heavens; no screams or cries for mercy in the warzone. Nothing. It must be a glitch; this can't be how it ends. The fight for dominance in humanity must mean something, right? It's all for something, right? An endless pit of emptiness caging our very existence can't be how it ends. Right?

Tarunika Venkatesan (17)

TEST GONE WRONG!

I don't know how it happened; all we were supposed to do was preserve his body for seven days. And that's what we did! We gathered the smartest people together and decided to find out what would happen if we froze a human's body. We did all the research and gathered the right materials. We tested on a lot of people. It worked perfectly. And now when we tried it on Samuel Stone it all went terribly wrong. It started when his body began to shake, then his skin turned blue. His mouth started foaming, and he turned into a wolf... An electric blue killing machine.

Ayanfeoluwa Adebusoye (11)

SUNSET

The sun hadn't risen in five years...
That's what we were told. That's what we believed. What I believed. Because one day five years ago time seemed to stop. Everyone including government officials, seemed to panic. Everyone in the country was evacuated into underground catacombs, the result of a war so horrible that it was agreed that any memory of it should be assigned to oblivion. Nobody left the catacombs Nobody knew what had happened.
Today I made a mistake... Now I know. Now I know why we were sent down here and I wish that I didn't know.

Skye Tomlinson (15)

THE GLITCH

The pitter-patter of rain drummed against my coat as I peered into the murmuring water. My flesh quivered on my bones as my reflection grinned at me. Trembling, I stretched my fingertips towards the rippling water. A gasp escaped my lips. Gaunt hands grasped my wrist as I plunged into darkness; my fingernails scrabbling futilely against the iron grip. Chains seemed to clasp my chest while walls from every direction pressed against me until...
Fresh air filled my lungs as I lay gasping beside the murmuring water and the pitter-patter of rain drummed against my coat.

Leyu Cheng (12)

THE GLITCH

They called me insane. They called me mad. They called me crazy. If only they knew... I was brought to a therapist, Dr Kimmy Harling. I met her on Monday. Pretty girl. Quite young, about twenty. Pink hair, probably dyed. But she was fake. One hundred percent fake. From her fake smile to those fake toenails sticking out of her sandals. Fake.. Fake.. Fake. Nothing in this world is real anymore, not to me... Not after 'the glitch'. The glitch. A science project gone wrong. Mr Jackson sure regretted giving us that assignment, especially as he was the one who died...

Thanisha Lalam (12)

THE MYSTERIOUS BOOK

As the alarm blared its unpleasant shriek, Emma reluctantly got out of bed. Rubbing her eyes, she turned to look at the clock. 8:55 - she was late for work! Rushing into the library, she stumbled upon an ancient-looking book on a dusty bookshelf. *This book doesn't belong in the sci-fi section*, she thought to herself as she was studying the book thoroughly. Blowing the dust off it, she was intrigued by the sight of it. The book exuded opulence from its cover, bound in luxurious leather that whispered beneath her eager fingertips. She simply had to read it...

Aanya Saxena (12)

DEAD POETS' SOCIETY

I quite often came to the lakes. Just to observe, nothing else. There were rumours that poets died here when the oceans rose. Only I could know that this was true as I sat atop the grave of Miss Dickinson, no headstone present. She had been a darling to speak to, but she'd put up a fight upon realising what I was. I'd carried her body, along with many others: Allan Poe, Keats, Ginsberg, you name them, I've buried them.
What I wasn't prepared for was that poets made lifelong friends even in their deaths. Ghosts... they were oddly comforting company.

Gray Silcock (16)

TIME SLIPPING

This is impossible. I strut through the pain of the past and look through the memories. I am the past. How? Shifting through time hurts more than a break-up. The spinning stopped and I flicked my chocolate brown, long hair dramatically up.
I want to go home, seeing little me playing at my childhood home is weird. I'm walking over to little me, the brown matted hair, my eyes red from crying and the two different-coloured socks made me tear up. I survived the orphanage. "Hello, I am..." Before I could introduce myself, I was back in my apartment.

Nikola Rejszel (15)

CUSTOMER SERVICE

A long sigh escapes my lips. I've been talking to this computer for an hour now and I'm still not any closer to solving my problem. I finally decide to give up and leave my desk when I hear a resonant ping. My phone flashes up with a message. Five words sending consecutive chills rolling down my spine. "You should not have left." How could they - I never sent my number did I? Closing my eyes thinking I must be dreaming, a sharp knock reverberates from the door. "Mum," I call out, "are we expecting anyone?"
There is no reply.

Janna Nabih (18)

THE BOY THAT CHANGED THE WORLD

I knocked over the first domino and watched as all the others fell one by one, it made me think- what would happen if one change in the world affected other things so easily?
I remembered the story of a boy, who stole some money online, it corrupted our society as we know it. He had hacked a bank's system to steal money but didn't shut down his laptop, his parents accessed the money, his siblings, grandparents, too much money was being taken which meant there was less money for other things, government, education, healthcare. One boy changed the world.

Misa Neville (16)

ETERNAL DAMNATION

All the clocks had stopped working. For a mere moment, reality had flickered. Seconds later, an aroma of decay submerged the air. A soulless figure began to materialise. It was *him*. The captor of everyone I had ever met. *You* all know him as Death.
He greeted me with a wicked smile and, without wasting any time, transformed the surroundings. We were then amongst the land of torment, where the sinful and sinister cry aloud. He called upon Satan to show us around. A glimpse of my new home. An afterlife of lurking in the Devil's playground.

Zainub Zulfikhar (18)

THE COMPASS PARADOX

I had been working tirelessly for this moment, following every path down every dead end. This should have worked! I couldn't accept that I was losing my mind. Subtly, I began to cry. Tears of pain, sadness, stress and despair crept down my face onto the cold oak floor. Then it began...
A flash of light danced across the pale walls, illuminating the faded images of a forgotten time. Then, the peculiar compass blinked into life; I followed along the final path, now with a sense of purpose in this strange, dying world. I stepped, with courage, into nothing.

Jacob Scott-Batey (15)

THE RISE OF THE SUN

My plastic duck alarm was screaming at me with that loud quack in my ear, but something felt deeply wrong.
Towering darkness still filled the empty claustrophobic room like a pall crawling its sly fingers into every corner. Outside the window, the dead world was plunged into a black abyss. No birds were heard. No wind was howling. No life was seen.
A minuscule glowing ember at the edge of my vision threw my disbelieving eyes to where the sun lay shrivelled and dying. The scorching heat once the light of the world slowly drained to the Earth's core.

Nivedita Patel (12)

THE CLOCK

Lilly woke up, sweat pouring down her face. Panicked, she looked around. She was still here, but she was somewhere else a second ago... She looked at the clock necklace the lady from the workshop gave her. Ever since then she kept having hallucinations. As if the world kept glitching and taking her back to the same place. The clock kept ticking in her head... *Tick, tick...*
And there she stood, in the same place. It was dark, but stars guided her through the narrow staircase until in front of her stood something she was dreading to see... The clock.

Naiara Lopez Antolin (12)

TECHNOLOGY LOST

It's like the world would never have been different. As I sat on my couch reading, the stereo playing Taylor Swift in the background, I wondered what life would've been like if technology was still around. If the glitch hadn't taken it away. Ancient stories had told us for years that they would disappear, but they were ignored. Shunned. Disgraced from society, but when it did actually happen they were blamed for the loss. The human race was set back years, only because of one blip in the space-time continuum, that lost us years of valuable research.

Rachel Horne (14)

THE GLITCH

12.11.23. 2am. East California.
The rocket went up and the debris came back down. A ball of fire came crashing back down as the ground shook, we stood in shock for we didn't know there was a glitch in the computer system. Within half an hour all the major cities of the world were destroyed by bombs and explosives, planes crashing into buildings and trains derailing and killing thousands. A glitch had spread across the world's computers and destroyed everything. It all started when I bought an unlicensed video game for my computer. It was a glitch.

Henry Wynne (12)

CRACKED

The ground started to quiver, the electrocuting jolts sent a shot of adrenaline through my veins. I staggered off the chair grasping onto the closest object, which happened to be the ancient door frame that was hanging onto the walls for dear life. My eyes examined the room desperate for something more imperishable to hold on to. The cracks tore apart like cake being cut by a baker.
I clutched onto the rusty frame, my fingers edging deeper and deeper into the sharp metal. My thoughts evaporated into terror, the cracks crept closer towards me. It was too late.

Sreelakshmi Payyana (15)

THE MUTATED VIRUS

I've heard about the disease but I never thought I would catch it. It was a mutated computer-generated virus that turned humans into robots.
I prayed my family didn't get it. I lay on my bed terrified of losing myself but the changes were happening rapidly. My hands felt numb. My body felt rigid. My olive skin was painfully transforming into metal. I stood up mechanically and saw my reflection glinting in the window. I felt like I was living a nightmare! I wanted to scream in fear but the only thing that came out of my mouth was... *beep!*

Arianne Clarke (11)

MAMI AND ME

I don't know where my sister is. Yesterday, Mami returned from the sea, wailing, her arms clutching empty air. Now, the sound of waves against the shore rakes against my ears, churning my stomach. But Mami wants me to swim. My bare toes touch the water; I shiver as I sink deeper into the waves. The darkness beckons from below, the light dims. I see Mami's face split into a vicious, victorious smile... Beside me on the seabed is my infant sister's body, wrapped in the shawl Mami carried her in, mouth open in a soundless scream.
Just like mine.

Julia Kaufholz (16)

THE GLITCH

Bang! I looked out the window. In the window, I noticed myself. My reflection moved, but I didn't. My soul was separated from me. My mother's soul went to the kitchen. Was my mother also separated? Perhaps I was dreaming. I went back to bed, hopefully everything would be fine soon. No, the same thing happened in the morning; maybe I was hallucinating. Not everyone could have the same hallucination though. I felt empty in this life without a soul. New York, the city that never sleeps, seemed to be asleep. What has this glitch done to humanity?

Isla Searancke (11)

GREYSCALE

No one noticed it at first. How were we to know? Day by day, it slowly faded. So gradual that it was almost impossible to tell, but it couldn't be denied anymore. An invisible void was feeding on our world. Claiming our colour for itself. What were once cerulean blues and crimson reds were now indistinguishable shades of grey. Colour was just a distant memory. Every day became excruciatingly similar. It made you wish that you had memorised every hue, every shade of sunset and yet, as much as you strained your mind, you could not picture anything but grey.

Evannah John (14)

THE INVADERS

It was another, ordinary day in Essex. The sun shone like it always did and the birds sang just like they did every day. But, something wasn't right...
A dark, deathly cloud of alien spaceships approached the city centre at great speed, dropping bombs like pennies out of a jar.
A siren made a deafening noise to warn unsuspecting citizens of the danger, but it was too late.
The ground shook and buildings collapsed all around.
Planes fell out of the sky and a giant orb inhaled everything for miles around.
The world was then silent.

Louis Ryan (12)

THE ADVENTURER

The sun hadn't risen for five years. Five years ago there was a freak accident which caused a massive explosion.
Dangerous gases swirled around and the world suddenly went dark.
Everyone went underground glad of the bunkers that were ready for hurricanes. Slowly the food supply ran out. People were starving but too afraid to leave their safe confines.
That leads us to today. I will be the adventurer. I will enter this new world to save my family. I have made plans for these five years so I take a step outside. The air is knocked from my lungs.

Lily Samuel (14)

THE TERROR OF THE FORBIDDEN APP

Michael groggily woke up to see an unknown mansion. It had crimson windows and Micheal was bemused. Just then, a raucous sound came. Startled, Michael ran away and saw him. The Glitch. A chandelier scared Michael so he dashed away. He saw rusted trinkets as he crept into another room. He then saw a terrible sight. This entity, appropriately named 'The Glitch', was killing a man and making him into a glitch. He then realised. This was the new app that he had installed. It was forbidden by many but he installed it. Just then, The Glitch came to him...

Nihalraj Dunde (10)

THE WITCH'S CAT

'We buried it, but it came back...' is what lit up my phone screen. I immediately replied, questioning what they were about. I impatiently waited whilst I listened as the storm battered the sky above me. After what felt like centuries, my friend replied back to me saying, 'The witch's cat', which only meant one thing - the black cat truly did belong to a witch. Suddenly lightning came crashing down into my garden, as I peered out of the window, I saw it. The cat limped towards my house with twigs tangled in its hair as my blood ran cold.

Ethan Reading (17)

FEAR'S FACE

The sun cascaded through my window, sprinkling my room with yellow diamonds. My sleep was robbed from me as I yawned. Wandering around my apartment suddenly I heard a scream outside my window. Curiosity gripped me as I rushed to lean outside it where I silently clamped my hand over my mouth. Screaming internally, I fell to the floor, shaking violently. Fear gripped my heart, I didn't dare to look outside again as I tried to calm myself. It must be a mistake. Feeling calmer I rose and looked out the window... to see hundreds of my faces grinning back...

Yasmin Aldiyar (14)

WHAT HAPPENED?

It was ready. The trap which could change history. The creature was like a green goblin slithering slowly and steadily. There was a slimy substance being left behind which seemed like gooey slime. The ufologists spectated in the dusty dry sand, but then, the mysterious creature was nowhere to be seen. Then, in the blink of an eye, two of the same creatures appeared. It was strange. As they got near the trap, it morphed back into one. When it got to the very tip of the trap, *clash!* The trap went off, but the alien wasn't moving. What happened?

Declan Rawlings (12)

THE APP

As Jamal sat on his bed, on a Sunday evening, he saw an app. But it had warnings of avoiding it. Since Jamal is untrustworthy, he still installed it, avoiding the warning. One day, when he was going home from school, he received a call. It was from the app, so he answered it.
"Hello?" asked Jamal.
"Hello Jamal, it's me, Uncle Taher."
"Hello Uncle," replied Jamal.
"Bye," said Taher.
Jamal was so confused, so he sat until he realized Uncle Taher was dead. Was it a prank or his ghost?

Afnanu Zzaman (11)

GONE

The world was in chaos as people began randomly tapping in and out of reality. One moment they were there, the next they vanished, only to reappear in a strange white room. No one knew how or why it happened, but it was clear that something was seriously wrong. People were terrified to leave their homes, fearing they would be the next ones to disappear. The white room was a mystery, and those who were unlucky enough to end up there never knew when they would return to reality. It was a strange and unsettling situation that had the whole world on edge.

Hafsa Ahmed Bhatti (15)

THE DAY THE CLOCKS CHANGED

The clocks had stopped. Why? No one knew. Until this day. After five years, the handles changed. Every device in the world glitched from whatever it was onto a screen with a man with a blank background. He was wearing a mask so he could not be recognised.
But what he said changed everything. He told everyone that we had to go to a random place. If we didn't, we would get hunted down and killed within an hour!
At the mysterious place people were then brainwashed into doing whatever this guy said. However, it didn't work on me...

Zara Bates (14)

LOST IN MY OWN MIND

My alarm didn't go off? While rushing for school, my whole body feels strange. I'm in the bathroom, splashing my face with water. Looking up at the mirror, I don't move but my reflection does. Who am I? Where am I? I enter class, this teacher looks identical to my great-great-grandma. Is it really her? The room's freezing, only a coal fire to heat us. I notice the blackboard states '1914' as I hear loud banging noises, making my heart skip a beat.
Abruptly I wake, am I in a vision? I begin pinching myself, I feel nothing.

Heidi Weston (15)

ROBOT INVASION

Absent-mindedly, I was travelling through time. I landed on a floor full of rubble. A figure was walking towards me. Quietly, I hid in the nearest closet. Then, an unrecognisable voice started speaking in an unknown language. I took my phone out of my pocket. I read the date: 'July 5015'. How was that possible? It was the year 2023 a minute ago! Suddenly, my phone made a loud ding sound. The door banged right open! it couldn't be... It was my robot friend, Ally holding a big, sharp knife. Just then I was back to my pink bedroom with Ally.

Summer Tsang (12)

THE WORLD GLITCH

After a day's work, I noticed a UFO hovering over my workplace. Rays of lights display our rebuilt, mechanical world being destroyed. The year 2103, humanity has advanced so much over the past century, but all of that hard labour has turned against us. Now, people are fleeing our current world, planet Mars. We've already destroyed one planet, now this is about to be destroyed too. The Government superiors have fled to the nearest galaxy, but their ships were halted mid-flight and exploded. I don't know what to do. No one knows what to do.

Taaseen Liton (14)

THE GLITCH

Five kids chatted happily to each other while walking into church. They each went and walked over to their parents and took a seat. "We are all thankful for this world and wish it never changes," says the vicar. He went to open his mouth to speak again but froze, nobody moved except the five children. The world had glitched.
That was six years ago... The five teenagers now walk up to the church and walk in silently, they sit in the same spot as six years ago.
Half of the world burned. Everybody unfreezes but nobody believes them.

Isabella Bremner (12)

ASLEEP

I look outside and see everything yet hear nothing. Thousands of individuals in the formation of a marching band walking down the road. They sound almost dead, making no noise, only focused on arriving at a destination. Confused, I asked what was going on. No response. They behaved like sleeping robots, being controlled by a higher status. Like the world was really just a simulation, a hologram, a sham. I felt eyes watching my every move. I felt crowded, fearful and nervous. I was terrified. Am I meant to be awake? Or is this a glitch in the system?

Numa Manzar (17)

FALLING

I stared at my body on the floor. The trail of crimson dotted through the snow seemed to shine like sequins in the moonlight - beautiful. My body grew paler. It's funny how snow has a way of settling the fires within, and had caused mine to go out. The figure next to me looked up at the cliff to where my friends were, all staring at what had seemed to brush all the pine tree's needles down, wiping off their cape of white and leaving their beautiful evergreen colour to shine with its dripping icicles.
"What happened?" it said.

Sylvia Tindale (12)

ARE WE AT THE END YET?

A fierce grip coiled around my upper arm and violently hurled me into a porcelain white room. It is time I faced the consequences of my actions. A sharp object pierced my neck, and I watched crimson-red blood emanate onto the colourless floor.
Wearily, my eyes fluttered open, and I found myself in a field of bloodshed, a scarlet maze. The place where it happened. My knuckles were bruised like violets, the vivid evocations came back to me in a blur. Our world has been a continuous loop of torture, despair, and isolation since they took control.

Bryony Boyce (14)

THE CHIP

A year ago, everything changed.
Years before that, the announcements started... "Get your kids the chip, protect them..." they claimed; now everyone has it or so they believe.
But I don't, they believe me dead, lost in the burning inferno that was my home. I lost my arm and the chip that day, but I gained everything. I gained freedom. I found the chip-less. Most of us have our chips for safekeeping but we have the power now. We will not be condemned to death with a click of a button; we are the rebellion, and we will fight.

Clarisse Marriott (15)

THE GLITCH

You will not believe how I died...
It began as I was awoken early in the morning, to a blood-curdling scream. I crept into my children's room to check they were alright. As I was going, they both sat bolt upright. Their heads (perfectly synchronised) turned to face me I was damp with sweat. I passed out. Next thing I knew, a nurse was treating a gaping wound on my head. "Every child in the world did the same," she whispered. "Who knew that app would cause so much harm?"
But it was too late for me, and the world...

Lyra Jordan (11)

THE GNOME

We buried it but it was back. Gnome. Fifteen years free of torture, now it's back for revenge. To steal spirits from innocent humans, trapping them for all eternity. I needed to reform the group. This was the only way to defeat it. I contacted Izzy and Ethan, informing Gnome was back. They quickly arrived at my home, we needed a plan.
After a while, we had it. Our spiritual bond was strong enough to break the curse. But Gnome knew our plan... Suddenly a shriek! Izzy! She vanished. Ethan too! But now, it was my doom... "Help me!"

Lilly-Mai Chase (13)

THE IVY

A scientist walks into a laboratory, dishevelled and anxious. He only came here to investigate the infestation of ivy, but lately felt as if something were watching him. Ignoring this feeling, he prepares a solution he believes will kill a sample of ivy. As he turns, the ivy sneakily moves out of its cage. Twisting around his leg, trapping him to the ground. He screams, paralysed. The scientist is engulfed by the ivy, his screams reverberating in the abandoned laboratory.
The ivy grows an inch. The world covered in ivy, growing inch by inch.

Raine Wong (16)

THE MYSTERIOUS RINGER

I was on my phone scrolling on TikTok. All of a sudden my phone began to ring. It wasn't someone I knew, they were named 'Anonymous Caller'. At first, I thought it could've been my mates playing a joke on me but when I answered... a creepy voice said, "I can see you." I hung up terrified and shaking. I accidentally dropped my phone and it smashed into pieces. I looked down in horror, as the broken phone began to receive a text message, through the cracked screen I read: 'I can still see you'.
I screamed...

Noah Van der Linden (13)

GLITCHING FUTURE

A sharp hue of violet and crimson glazes over my eyes as I stare at the sky crumbling down over us. Voices calling my name from all around me, being stretched out and carried like songbirds echoing in the trees, only this time with a distorted frequency. I turn around to see myself, an older version with slightly longer hair, sparkling like phosphenes. Her face is pixelated and she's screaming at me yet I can't hear. I look down and my hands start to slowly fade, my vision goes black like I'm floating into a dark void. Maybe I am...

Ameerah Ghariani (16)

MIDNIGHT STRIKES

Ashlyn knew that at midnight all would change, the moment when everything just stopped. The world was on the brink of something big and she could feel it. The girl was ready, prepared for whatever came next. She stocked up on supplies, made sure her weapons were ready and fortified her safe house. She sat in the darkness, waiting for the clock to strike twelve. As she waited, she heard a roar coming from outside, a sound that made her blood run cold. The world had changed, nothing would be the same. *Beep.* The clock had struck midnight.

Kenuli Don (14)

TIME TURNER

Cold air chilled my bones, foggy voices echoed around the room. I lay daydreaming. I was in a... Ow! A small girl dressed neatly in a pink, linen frock was vigorously attacking me with her hairbrush.
I sat up rubbing my arm and with the other felt under the bed for my smiley face slippers. *Ahh, got them,* I thought as I tugged something fluffy from the floor. Wait! My floor is covered in carpet? That cheap type from that dodgy shop on the corner.
That's when I realised this wasn't 2023. This must be some kind of glitch...

Zea Windett (11)

THE IPHONE 16 VIRUS

It is the year 2024 and everyone was excited about the arrival of the iPhone 16s, little did everyone know that it contained a deadly secret...
The iPhone 16 is the new iPhone, with many new functions but with one strange difference, it has deadly viruses in it.
The iPhone 16 has something called the zyroghlobic virus which can cause a person - in the radius of 1cm (about 0.39 in) - 10000m (about 6.21 mi) - to be ripped apart by their own heart rapidly enlarging.
I can confirm that this is true, and I am now the only known survivor.

Dylan Carroll (13)

THE DAY IT CAME

We buried it but it was back! The thing we all feared was back! It seeped out its hideous black tongue rolled around in its mouth. "Run!" I screamed as the monster swallowed its first victim.
The beast gave a loud cry and at that moment a platoon of spaceships came. I ran, but they were in pursuit. They followed me as I ran. The calamity and screaming were everywhere; people were throwing their arms in the air as they were annihilated. Then it was my turn, all turned black, a swirling portal appeared as I was sucked into it.

Anton Kaplunov (11)

TIME IS GONE

I awoke that morning, darkness surrounding me. Nothing to see. Time was gaining fast but nothing changed, it was as if the world had stopped, except for me. The breeze did not come through the morning window. Confused, I clambered out of the covers - which had seemed like they were sewn to the bed - and attempted to open the door, but it wouldn't move. Could it be locked?
No. There was a key dangled on the floor next to my feet. But for the amount of effort that I tried, the keys wouldn't lift with my hand. What was happening?

Sadie McSharry (12)

THE DOWNLOADED APP

James was bored and thought of downloading an app. Little did he know it would be a crisis. It was about when you will die which seemed silly. Notifications said he would never leave this game which he thought was a joke. His friends and James played the game. One of his friends failed and immediately they found he was dead.
Time went by until every person in the world got this installed on their phone. People were dying, which seemed weird.
No one could remove this game. Finally, James found that he was the master of this game.

Philia Sanoj (13)

REFLECTIONS UNBOUND

My reflection moved, but I didn't. It was just a split second, but it sent a chill down my spine. Confused, I blinked and looked again, only to find my reflection frozen in place. Heart racing, I cautiously reached out, and to my shock, my hand passed right through the mirror. Panic washed over me as I realised I had stumbled across a glitch in the matrix. With each passing moment, reality seemed to warp and twist around me. Unsure of what to do, I took a deep breath and stepped forward, ready to uncover the mysteries that awaited me.

Lena Wilczewska (12)

REVERSED WORLD?

I'm not the hero of this story but it's a warning of the future and for survival.
It started when I stepped outside and to my dismay, the right side of my street was a mirror image of the left. People gathered around the spectre. I noticed cracks in the mirror, where a horrific wasteland appeared. Everything was dead, a shell of its former life. The local shopkeeper put his hand through the crack and to our shock he was sucked in, with a shriek. There was silence, he had been sucked into the vengeful, fearful reversed world.

Theo Bass (13)

THE GATE GLITCH

Whilst everyone's asleep, the animals at Worksop Wildlife Park are just up for a long day. John is the strongest, most powerful big cat around. Bruce and Reggie are from the Australian section and are both wombats. All the animals love Jack because he loves them.

Then all the gates suddenly opened!

The first to notice was John. Who charged out expecting applause not screaming. Next came Reggie and Bruce who only left for a minute until Jack ushered them back in. John was lassoed and secured in his cage. Everyone was safe.

Oscar Morgan (12)

THE DEAD

I ran with my sister's hand in the palm of my hand. It was raining: this didn't stop us. Some lingering shadows were chasing us; lightning struck right in front of us but that didn't stop us. I saw an open door, I grasped my sister's hand and sped in. I went in, locking the door as fast as possible. I blocked the door with furniture and sat down in a chair. Global warming created this virus. Turned these people into dead-living creatures, bloodthirsty zombies. We need to get weapons to... Something banged on the door...

Safwan Mohammed Sadiq (11)

DEATH'S COLLECTION

I was supposed to be safe, for at least another month. That was if the thought of my inevitable demise didn't wipe me out first. I began to have that feeling in my gut, as if my organs were twisting and turning, trying to warn me of the danger lying ahead and save me from this gruesome end. The deafening explosions started, and I could hear the silent sound of screams in the distance. My knees dropped to the grassy floor as I drew my last agonising breath.
'If we don't end war, war will end us' H G Wells.

Sasha Cox (16)

GONE WITH THE GLITCH

It was an ordinary day until I heard it. My life's greatest fear. The glitch alarm. The glitchy blare of the alarm echoed through the city. There was a mischievous glitch that brought havoc upon the digital realm. But something was wrong with it, the ones that we know are colourful. This one was white. Then it hit me. I read about this once, it is one that makes people vanish without a trace. It came closer. And closer. Suddenly it was gone. As much as I screamed no one would respond. Then I realised, I was gone with the glitch...

Karshmika Pushparajah (13)

A FUTURE OF FIRE AND ICE

Solar flares. Futures destroyed. Technology, a broken dream. A wasteland of metal and lifeless wire lies beyond me, only now I realise how addicted we were, how dependent we were. Dust heavy in the air as I walk through the now-fallen city.
Deafening screams invade the silence of shock, fire raging in my vision as it claims the Earth. Never did we think we were walking on ice, that someday it might crack. And as it melts, we drown in the icy reality. Technology was our everything. But the ice has broken, and we struggle to swim.

Rosa Kelly (14)

THE RETURN OF THE LOST

The past is becoming the future. The reminder of what ruined our country 84 years ago, what ruined me. Fire, bangs, screaming. Souls built over like their presence never existed. I was never the same.
The world shakes. The sky becomes instantly dark and rain plummets from the sky. I hear thunder... or is it thunder? I hear the squelching under my steps as I fear to look down. My heart is thumping yet am I just overthinking? My vision blurs as the rain covers my eyes, The bones we buried are uncovered as death lines my path home.

Maija Adamson (16)

A DAY GONE ROGUE

It's a day that's gone rogue. It's gone out of control. You'll never guess how it happened though. Everything started off normally until I got to the second period, you see. I was just minding my own business when everything spiralled. It was because I'd run into Mrs Fitzgerald. You can't even fathom how much I cried because this encounter was worse than witnessing someone dying.
Alas, my day went rogue. It just went out of control. And now you know how it happened. Second period was a nightmare, you see.

Taifa Rawza (12)

THE HORRORS OF WAR

With a grump and a thump, the lifeless soldiers marched towards the ghastly battlefield drunk with fatigue. However, at the back of the squadron, two lively, spirited soldiers trailed behind the drowsy so-called glorious heroes, but in their eyes all they were focused on was going home and seeing their families again. The squelching of their boots and the coughing from the gas, until all was silent, but then... *Whizz! Whizz! Whizz!* A trio of bullets flew past them, hitting the soldiers. As they fell, there was only panic...

Harry Andrews (12)

SKY OF HELICOPTERS

After a tiring day, Marie placed down her tea and finally laid her legs to rest upon the table, where she began to let her eyes wander towards the window. Somewhat oddly, the stars seemed to aggressively twinkle, more reminiscent of a sky full of helicopters; this disturbed her eyes, so she rolled down her blinds. She opened her diary and began to write of her day, she had been so invested in writing she forgot to drink her tea. But, when she looked up, it was gone. Her blinds were open, and her diary was empty. What just happened?

George Cannon (14)

THE GOVERNMENT'S GLITCH

The TV was soaring as the news came on. The news reporter claimed there had been a glitch in the government but what that meant remained a mystery. Thousands and thousands of questions ran through my head. I couldn't think straight but before they could hand out any more information the town was in the midst of a blackout. Everyone ran outside their homes as if they were being controlled but I didn't, I searched for the time but all the clocks were deactivated as was my phone. I looked out my window. Everything was gone.

Esme Loughlin (14)

FAMILY MYSTERY

A present has been passed on, you got yours for your 16th birthday but your mum decided to hide it. When your parents were out you got the idea to look for it. After looking around for what felt like years, you find it in the back of your mum's wardrobe. The enchanted spine practically begs you to open the book. But when you do everything starts floating, you shut it instantly and everything drops. When you open the book to a different page everything but you stops. What kind of book is this? How did your ancestors get it?

Aleksandra Malinowska (15)

THE ALIENS ARE HERE

It was quite a normal day for Harry, he was watching TV while feeding his dog. Harry loved his dog; he didn't know what he would do without him. But this normal day turned into a not-so-normal day. Harry was watching the news on the TV, and they were talking about aliens coming to Earth. "Aliens coming to Earth?" Harry exclaimed. He didn't know what he was going to do in his last moments on Earth. But finally, he decided that he was going to embrace death and spend his last minutes with his dog.

Ali Waraich (12)

THE SWITCH

Max woke up, blinded by a mysterious blue light. It felt as if he was bound to the bed, unable to move. As his eyes adjusted to the light, he realised he wasn't in his room. On the beds next to him, green alien figures were similarly bound to the beds. Max lifted his head and saw feet beyond his gurney. That's when he realised... he was not in his body. Elsewhere, in Max's apartment, his eyes opened, and he realised he wasn't staring into the blue light for the first time since he arrived on Earth.

Muhammed Fuaad (18)

A CRACK IN TIME

As the power outlet stopped, time did too. As Rose woke from her slumber she saw no one move. Silent as a mouse, she pondered in her head. Rose could do what she wanted to. She went to theme parks, trampolines but she realised there was no one to do it with. She needed to go to the centre of the universe. So Rose packed her bags and left. She went into the space station and pressed the button. Rose landed in her own dimension. So where did she come from? Could she call it her own? "I miss you," she said.

Sofia Lo Bue (11)

WORD-SWORDS FALLING

It's not because I'm young or from a broken home. Maybe I just fight because I don't know where I belong.
At that moment it was hard to see if I was the fool, or if they were a thief.
It lasted twenty minutes, but it felt like an eternity. I was the diamond they left in the dust and the word-swords fell to pierce inside me.
These scars I will no longer hide as there is a glitch in my mind at heart, preventing me from hiding them.
The injuries have healed. It's words I remember.

Victoria Cicha (16)

THE GLITCH

I knew I shouldn't have but I couldn't help it. I slowly wandered into the house along with my friends. The house was damaged and unilluminated. We were all appointed to a section of the house. The bathrooms became my priority. Now it was time to see if the rumours were true. I slowly approached the mirror.
I wished I could have run out of there, but something came over me. I was stuck. I felt a weight holding me to the floor. I began to just stare.
Little did I know it would end with me dead...

Zoe Ojo (12)

THE GLITCH

Every clock had terminated except one. Time was streaming away. Water was trickling down my face as if I was a plant in a downpour. The sun hadn't risen for years. There was no light anywhere. It was just pitch dark!
It was like I was time travelling! I felt so intimidated and isolated.
I stopped breathing for a minute and I remembered that there was this one man that I knew and he told me that this would last forever. I decided to sleep. What was the point of waking up?
Why is this happening?

Nazneen Dauhoo (13)

THE PRINCE WHO NEVER BECAME KING

At a very young age, Neymar Jr, a young, skilful masterclass football player destroyed La Liga with Barcelona. Scoring goals alongside Messi and Suarez.
A couple of years later Neymar began to reach his prime. Scoring as top goal scorer in the UCL and winning the UCL with Barcelona.
Under all this, his mental health and injury-prone status ruined him. He could continue playing for Barcelona or accept tonnes of money from PSG. He chose the money. A talent who wasted his career. And the rest was history.

Robert Burn (13)

FLIPPED

When I woke, I immediately felt it. Something was wrong. I looked around my room trying to place my finger on what it was. Everything looked the same - as far as I could tell. And then I noticed it. My door was the other way round; my scissors left-handed; my books, all the other way round. Slowly, I made my way downstairs. I saw my mum, the same except she was using her left hand to eat. She smiled at me. I wanted to join her except I knew it wasn't really her. People can't come back from the dead.

Esme Percival (15)

THE BUTTON

Ronaldo was searching through his diseased father's old box when he found a pocket watch with a button. He clicked the button...
His brother froze, so did everything else around him, he pressed it again and everything resumed. He used this new watch to do many tricks and stunts, taking advantage of the power to freeze time. But then, while time was paused, Ronaldo dropped the watch and glared down as it fell to its end. He picked it up and pressed it but nothing happened, time was paused forever...

Mahdi Rahman (11)

THE TIME GLITCH

It was a normal day in a normal town. The birds were singing and time was ticking. Sophie was walking to school. Step, step, step went her shoes on the ground, as the hands of time spun around. Sophie checked her watch. 8:46am. Four minutes to get to school, she started to sprint. 8:47, 8:48, 8:49. She checked her watch again. Still 8:49. She checked again expecting her watch to show her she was late. The birds stopped singing, the cars stopped mid-drive, the hands of time came to a jolting stop. But why?

Jack Taylor (12)

THE GLITCH

The clock stood silently still. We were out of time. How could we fix it now?
I was stupid, why would I get that app? This wasn't my room, it was pitch black. The horrific sense of fear engulfed me. A violent shiver fell down my spine.
Was the description of the app right? A noise came from the near distance. This is where I knew I was about to meet my fate. The creature scuttled closer. This was the moment I was going to die.
I wish I never got that app. I warn you all, never get it.

Hannah Firth (14)

THE VIRUS OF DREAMS

I scream and thrash, the bed quilt wrapped around my limbs, like a prisoner. I am a prisoner. I am a prisoner of my dreams. Through my room the figures move. I reach out to touch them, but my fingers float through the apparition. I squeeze my eyes closed and rub my temples, praying that this is just another nightmare, but of course, it isn't, it hasn't been for the past ten years. I look out from my window and see others struggling too. We all have the same fate - and that fate never leaves us.

Rowan Brown (13)

THE GLITCH

Chasse Owens, was a normal boy in a normal school. As Chasse walked down the hallway the clocks froze. Everyone was frozen. It was silent. The lights flickered as the mirror down the hall shimmered. As Chasse looked in the mirror the lights flickered and shut off. The silent hallways suddenly became loud again. People laughed and giggled, walking through the Stateworths Academy doors. Chasse froze. Was this a joke? Chasse was the only one who saw this? What was it? A time freeze? A dream? A glitch...?

Lacey-Mae Banks (13)

A CRACK IN THE SYSTEM

It all started with an earthquake. The earthquake of doom. A year ago a large earthquake occurred, but nothing was catastrophic about it. Everyone chose to ignore it. But who could have known how much change it brought to us? A month ago it was blue trees and just yesterday grass rivers. Nothing makes sense. You can trust no one. Nowhere is safe. The sea is now the sky. The world is split into islands. Our whole world changed, our lives all changed. Just because of an error in the system...

Meenakshi Rapally (16)

PAUSED

All the clocks stopped like the world had glitched. The minute I woke up I went to check my phone. The time wasn't on there either. The world around me stopped moving, I didn't know what time it was or even what day it was. What was I going to do? It felt like the world paused and I was the only living thing left. I had to find out what was going on! Is this the future? I didn't know where to start. Which way should I go first? The whole world had stopped, all apart from me...

Chloe Keevil-Hillier (13)

THE GLITCH

It was one cold winter's morning. I uploaded this song onto Spotify then there was a loud bang on my front door which made me jump. So, I wondered if it was one of my family members. When I got to the door to see who it was no one was there. So, I shut the door and went to upload the song onto Spotify then suddenly, I heard a loud bang on my front door which made me jump again. So, I wondered if it was my family members... That meant I was in 'the glitch'.

Kyle Thomas (18)

THE GLITCH

I was at a theme park with my friend Clara, we were so excited to be there for the biggest ride. As we got on, I felt my nerves kick in. Suddenly, I felt like I had woken up from a dream, but really, I was soaring through the air at a rapid speed. I can only remember crashing through a mirror to see green grass and purple skies. Somehow, I was back with Clara at the end of the roller coaster. She gave me a high five with the same hand as me... Was this her mirror?

Eliza Wood (11)

THE GLITCH SWITCH

It shouldn't have happened this way. Why did this happen today of all days? A parasite appeared. It took them. Murders followed. So why is a child shaking in front of me crying? Glitching. This isn't right, I want to scream my heart out. I don't want to be the reason a child dies but they are suffering, I need to, I need to pull the trigger... 3, 2, 1... *Bang!* I did it. I killed the child. The glitch takes over. Goodbye, I'm sorry.

Heather Chandler (18)

THE TIME STOPPED

I woke up to an alarm and checked my phone but realised the time had stopped and the sun wasn't rising. I got up and didn't think any more of it. I went to the bathroom and brushed my teeth, noticing my reflection was moving on its own. I yelled out a loud scream of terror, asking myself if this was a dream. I went to the living room and opened up the window for some fresh breeze realising portals had ripped in the sky, causing a glitch in the matrix.

Leah-Jade Abraham (16)

FINAL MOMENT

I was cold. Lifeless bodies spread around me dressed in military gear. There was not one man on his two feet... until I got onto mine.
I walked around a hellish landscape - my head was dominated by one thought... *Keep walking*, a voice seemed to whisper to me as I started to collapse onto the ground.
I felt pain tear through my body as I flew into the air. When I rushed to open my eyes, I saw the road and the car that had just hit me.

Edward Hartlebury (13)

MONSTER UNDER THE BED

A long growl reverberated through the house. I had forgotten to feed it before, just once. Then I had no father. Legend has it that one unlucky pet owner would have a monster. And it was me. I can still picture streaks of blood on the walks, the sharp gruesome scent choking me. Now it was my sister. The monster's bloodshot eyes nearly gave me a heart attack. Suddenly I heard the monster come downstairs. It hadn't come down before... Why now?

Ayaan Rehman (11)

THE AI ATTACK

It was the summer of 7023 when all the power to the world went out and the older versions of the AI robots relied on the power to work so they all powered off for good. Because of this the newer versions attacked us.
For the last month, we have been at war with them. 10,552 people were found dead and 11 were found injured.
It was over a few days ago. Me and a few friends were the only survivors and we now must rebuild the world.

Izzie Holland (13)

THE WEIRDEST DAY TO BE ALIVE!

One day, me and my best friend Amy were playing on a nearby playground, when I asked her to race. Knowing she would say yes (which she did) we began to run. Suddenly, all sightings around me vanished. "Rebecca, what is going on?" Amy exclaimed, with a confused expression on her face.
A million thoughts raced through my mind. The only thing that could have happened was that the world had a glitch. But how is that possible?

Rebecca Morris (11)

TIME-SAVER

It all began on a busy road. Darren was crossing the road with his new Beats headphones. Darren was too busy listening to a new song on Spotify. As he looked up, he saw a car coming at him at full speed. Darren was so terrified as the car was five feet away from him. As it crossed time had stopped. What was going on? Darren was so happy as he survived a car accident, but he learned to live like this for the rest of his life.

Nivain Jayawardana (11)

TODAY

Tara and I were on the sofa on Sunday. It was that Sunday that changed my life forever. I was feeling a bit peckish so I went to the kitchen. Tara was asleep and I didn't want to wake her so I tiptoed quietly. Luckily I did because I heard a small sound, almost like a whistle, above the room. It gradually got louder and louder until I knew what it was but I needed to act fast. I got Tara as fast as I could...

Vaidehi Sonigra (12)

YOUNG WRITERS INFORMATION

We hope you have enjoyed reading this book – and that you will continue to in the coming years.

If you're the parent or family member of an enthusiastic poet or story writer, do visit our website **www.youngwriters.co.uk/subscribe** and sign up to receive news, competitions, writing challenges and tips, activities and much, much more! There's lots to keep budding writers motivated!

If you would like to order further copies of this book, or any of our other titles, then please give us a call or order via your online account.

Young Writers
Remus House
Coltsfoot Drive
Peterborough
PE2 9BF
(01733) 890066
info@youngwriters.co.uk

Join in the conversation!
Tips, news, giveaways and much more!

YoungWritersUK YoungWritersCW
youngwriterscw youngwriterscw

SCAN TO WATCH THE GLITCH VIDEO!